Contents

The Great Dog Trainer

Gus loved to go
to Grandpa's house.
At Grandpa's house,
there was a dog
named Skipper
who waited for Gus
at the gate.

At Grandpa's house,
there was a ditch
Gus could jump across.
At Grandpa's house,
there was a wheelbarrow
Gus could fill
with stones and grass
and sticks and mud.

Most of all,
Gus loved Grandpa's house
because at Grandpa's house
there was Grandpa.

Gus's mother said
goodbye to Grandpa.
"Be a good boy," she told Gus.
"Don't make a big mess
for Grandpa to clean up."
Then she kissed Gus
and drove away.

Gus and Skipper
played in Grandpa's yard.
They took turns jumping
across Grandpa's ditch.
Gus jumped.
Skipper jumped.
Gus jumped.
Skipper jumped.
Gus jumped.

But this time
Gus didn't jump
quite far enough.
Most of Gus
didn't get wet.
Just one foot
and one ankle
and one shin
and one knee.

Next, Gus pushed
Grandpa's wheelbarrow
around the picnic table.
Skipper chased it.
He barked and nipped
at the wheelbarrow
as if it were
a squirrel or a magpie.

Then Gus led Skipper
to Grandpa's back porch.
"Skipper is hungry,"
Gus told Grandpa.

"Well, feed him!"
Grandpa said.
Grandpa went
to water his corn.

Gus opened the bin
of dry dog food.
"Here, Skipper!"
Gus threw a piece
of dog food into the air.
Skipper tried to catch it,
but he missed.
Gus threw another piece
of dog food into the air.
This time Skipper caught it!

Maybe Gus could train Skipper
to be a circus dog.
Maybe he could train Skipper
to be a famous dog-food catcher.
Training Skipper was hard work.

Gus kept throwing dog food
into the air.
Sometimes Skipper caught it.
Sometimes Skipper missed.
Gus threw the dog food
higher and higher.
Skipper wagged his tail
harder and harder.

Then Grandpa came in.
"What happened here?"
he asked.

Gus looked.

There was no more dog food
in the bin.

But there was dog food
everywhere else.

Dog food on the floor.

Dog food on Grandpa's chair.

Dog food on Skipper's chair.

Dog food on Skipper's back.

Gus waited to see
what Grandpa would say.

Maybe now Grandpa wouldn't let
Gus be a famous dog trainer.

Grandpa handed Gus a broom.

"Well, sweep it off of here!"
he said.

Gus swept and swept.
Sweeping was fun.
Maybe he would be
a famous sweeper.

When Gus's mother
came to get him,
she said to Grandpa,
"I hope Gus was a good boy.
I hope he didn't make
a big mess."

"Oh, no," Grandpa said.
"My floor out back
 has never been cleaner!"

The Lost Car

Another day, Gus and his father
went to Grandpa's house.
Gus's father sat down to work
at Grandpa's picnic table.
Skipper guarded the yard.
He kept it safe
from squirrels and magpies.
Gus went shopping with Grandpa.

Gus and Grandpa went
to the hardware store.
Gus helped Grandpa
pick out nails.

Gus and Grandpa went
to the pet store.
Gus helped Grandpa
pick out a new bowl
for Skipper.

Gus and Grandpa went
to the grocery store.
They hurried to
the bakery department
for free samples.
Today the free samples were
chocolate doughnut holes
rolled in white sugar.

They each took one.
"We should only
eat one doughnut hole,"
Grandpa said.
But they both ate another.
"That's enough for us,"
Grandpa said.
But they each ate
one more.

Gus and Grandpa got
free samples
for Skipper, too.
They got a bag
of free dog bones
in the meat department.
They bought some groceries:
a jar of popcorn,
and pancake mix,
and chocolate milk,
and macaroni.
"Okay," Grandpa said.
"Time to go home
and check up on
your daddy."

In the parking lot,
Grandpa couldn't find his car.
He and Gus walked up
one row of cars
and down another.
They saw one gray car
that looked like Grandpa's.
But it had a baby seat inside.

They saw another gray car
that looked like Grandpa's.
But it had a dog inside
that was not Skipper.
"Maybe my car
got tired of waiting
and went on home,"
Grandpa said.
But he frowned.

Then Gus remembered.
"I know!
We parked by the pet store!"
Gus and Grandpa
went back to the pet store.
They saw Grandpa's gray car
parked right in front.
It did not have a baby seat in it.
It did not have a wrong dog.

Grandpa said,
"I am going to get
a big ball of yarn.
I will tie one end to the car.
I will take the other end
with me.
Then when I want
to find my car,
I will follow the yarn.
Better yet, Gus,
I will always take you
with me."

At Grandpa's house,
Gus's father gave him a hug.
"You were gone a long time,"
he said.
"Did you get lost?"

"Nope," Gus said.
He and Grandpa did not get lost.
The car got lost.
But then Gus found it.

The Birthday Party

Gus and Grandpa
had almost
the same birthday.
Grandpa's birthday was
August 4. He was seventy.
Gus's birthday was
August 6. He was seven.
So on August 5
they shared one big party.

They baked one big cake.

They frosted the top
of one layer.
They ate some frosting
from the can.
They frosted the top
of the other layer.
They ate more frosting
from the can.
But they could not frost
the sides.
The can was empty.
Then they decorated the cake
with sprinkles
and M&Ms.
They put lots and lots
of colored candles
on top.

Gus's mother and father
came to the party.
Skipper came to the party, too.
But he ate free dog bones
instead of cake.

Gus opened lots of presents.
He got a toy train
and a blue sweater
and a book about birds.

Grandpa opened lots of presents.
He got a warm jacket
and a video of an opera
and a book about wine.

Then Gus gave his present
to Grandpa.
Grandpa gave his present
to Gus.

Gus opened his knobby package.
"A dog-food scoop!"

Grandpa opened his lumpy package.
"A big ball of yarn!"

They both began to laugh.
Skipper barked.
"What are you two laughing about?"
Gus's father asked.

Gus and Grandpa
just kept on laughing,
and Skipper kept on barking
and thumping his tail.